A Beginning-to-Read Book

Hanukkah

by Mary Lindeen

NORWOOD HOUSE PRESS

DEAR CAREGIVER, The *Beginning to Read—Read and Discover* books provide emergent readers the opportunity to explore the world through nonfiction while building early reading skills. The text integrates both common sight words and content vocabulary. These key words are featured on lists provided at the back of the book to help your child expand his or her sight word recognition, which helps build reading fluency. The content words expand vocabulary and support comprehension.

Nonfiction text is any text that is factual. The Common Core State Standards call for an increase in the amount of informational text reading among students. The Standards aim to promote college and career readiness among students. Preparation for college and career endeavors requires proficiency in reading complex informational texts in a variety of content areas. You can help your child build a foundation by introducing nonfiction early. To further support the CCSS, you will find Reading Reinforcement activities at the back of the book that are aligned to these Standards.

Above all, the most important part of the reading experience is to have fun and enjoy it!

Sincerely,

Shannon Cannon

Shannon Cannon, Ph.D.
Literacy Consultant

Norwood House Press • P.O. Box 316598 • Chicago, Illinois 60631
For more information about Norwood House Press please visit our website at
www.norwoodhousepress.com or call 866-565-2900.
© 2019 Norwood House Press. Beginning-to-Read™ is a trademark of Norwood House Press.
All rights reserved. No part of this book may be reproduced or utilized in any form or by any
means without written permission from the publisher.

Editor: Judy Kentor Schmauss
Designer: Lindaanne Donohoe

Photo Credits:
Shutterstock, cover, 1, 3, 6-7, 12-13, 14-15, 18-19, 20-21, 22-23, 27;
iStock, 8, 9, 10-11, 16-17, 25-25, 26, 28-29; Alamy, 4-5

Library of Congress Cataloging-in-Publication Data
Names: Lindeen, Mary, author.
Title: Hanukkah / by Mary Lindeen.
Description: Chicago : Norwood House Press, 2018. | Series: A beginning to
  read book.
Identifiers: LCCN 2018004463 (print) | LCCN 2018017309 (ebook) | ISBN
  9781684041725 (eBook) | ISBN 9781599539072 (library edition : alk. paper)
Subjects: LCSH: Hanukkah—Juvenile literature.
Classification: LCC BM695.H3 (ebook) | LCC BM695.H3 L56 2018 (print) | DDC
  296.4/35—dc23
LC record available at https://lccn.loc.gov/2018004463

Hardcover ISBN: 978-1-59953-907-2   Paperback ISBN: 978-1-68404-163-3

December

M	T	W	T	F	S	S
1	2	3	4	5	6	7
8	9	10	11	12	13	14
15	16	17	18	19	20	21
22	23	24	25	26	27	28
29	30	31				

Hanukkah is a winter holiday.

It comes in December.

Hanukkah lasts for eight days and nights.

It's called the Festival of Lights.

People light candles for Hanukkah.

The candles are in special holders.

One candle is lit on the first night.

Two are lit on the second night.

Three are lit on
the third night.

One more is lit
each night until
all the candles
are lit.

Blue and white are Hanukkah colors.

What blue and white things do you see?

Families and friends celebrate together.

They sing special songs.

They eat special foods.

These pancakes are a special treat.

They are made with potatoes.

These doughnuts are a special treat, too.

They have jelly in them!

Some kids play games.

They spin special tops.

Families give each other gifts.

Kids often get coins as gifts.

The coins are chocolate!

These special days are full of love and joy.

Happy Hanukkah!

...READING REINFORCEMENT...

CRAFT AND STRUCTURE

To check your child's understanding of the organization of the book, recreate the following chart on a sheet of paper. Read the book with your child, and then help him or her fill in the diagram using what they learned. Work together to complete the chart by writing words or ideas from the book that tell details about the main idea of Hanukkah:

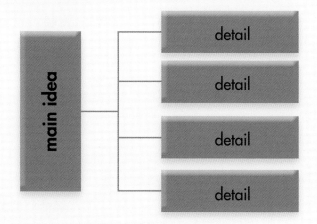

VOCABULARY: Learning Content Words

Content words are words that are specific to a particular topic. All of the cont words for this book can be found on page 32. Use some or all of these conte words to complete one or more of the following activities:

- Provide several clues as to the meaning of each word. Have your child gue the word.

- Write the words on slips of paper. Put them in a bowl. Have your child dra a slip of paper and use the word in a sentence.

- Have your child put the words into categories and then tell you what the categories are.

- Have your child cut out two pictures in magazines that will help him or her remember the meaning of the word.

- Have your child find smaller words or word parts within the words.

FOUNDATIONAL SKILLS: Multisyllabic words

Multisyllabic words are words that have more than one syllable; for example, *Hanukkah* has 3 syllables. Have your child identify the number of syllables in the words below. Then help your child find other multisyllabic words in this book.

Hanukkah	winter	holiday	festival
candles	families	celebrate	pancakes
potatoes	jelly	doughnuts	chocolate

CLOSE READING OF INFORMATIONAL TEXT

Close reading helps children comprehend text. It includes reading a text, discussing it with others, and answering questions about it. Use these questions to discuss this book with your child.

- How many nights does Hanukkah last?
- Why do you think Hanukkah is also called The Festival of Lights?
- Which Hanukkah activities sound like fun to you? Why?
- How is Hanukkah similar to other holidays? How is it different?
- What do you think is the most interesting thing about Hanukkah? Why?
- Why might some of the foods people eat on Hanukkah be special?

FLUENCY

Fluency is the ability to read accurately with speed and expression. Help your child practice fluency by using one or more of the following activities:

- Reread this book to your child at least two times while he or she uses a finger to track each word as it is read.
- Read the first sentence aloud. Then have your child reread the sentence with you. Continue until you have finished the book.
- Ask your child to read aloud the words they know on each page of this book. (Your child will learn additional words with subsequent readings.)
- Have your child practice reading this book several times to improve accuracy, rate, and expression.

••• Word List •••

Hanukkah uses the 84 words listed below. *High-frequency words* are those words that are used mc often in the English language. They are sometimes referred to as sight words because children nee to learn to recognize them automatically when they read. *Content words* are any words specific a particular topic. Regular practice reading these words will enhance your child's ability to read wi greater fluency and comprehension.

High-Frequency Words

a	each	last(s)	see	two
all	eat	made	some	until
and	first	more	the	what
are	for	of	them	white
as	get	often	these	with
blue	give	on	they	you
called	have	one	things	
come(s)	in	other	three	
day(s)	is	people	together	
do	it	play	too	

Content Words

candle(s)	families	happy	lit	specia
celebrate	Festival	holders	love	spin
chocolate	foods	holiday	night(s)	third
coins	friends	it's	pancakes	tops
colors	full	jelly	potatoes	treat
December	games	joy	second	winter
doughnuts	gifts	kids	sing	
eight	Hanukkah	light(s)	songs	

••• About the Author

Mary Lindeen is a writer, editor, parent, and former elementary school teacher. She has written more than 100 books for children and edited many more. She speciali. in early literacy instruction and books for young readers, especially nonfiction.

••• About the Advisor

Dr. Shannon Cannon is an elementary school teacher in Sacramento, California. She has served as a teacher educator in the School of Education at UC Davis, where she also earned her Ph.D. in Language, Literacy, and Culture. As a member of the clinical faculty, she supervised pre-service teachers and taught elementary methods courses in reading, effective teaching, and teacher action research.